The Many Marvellous Adventures of Winnie and Her Wonderful Wheelchair

David R Morgan

Illustrated by Anna Semenova

Dedication

*For Bex and Toby,
who are magical
and marellous,
And for Sue who
knows this too,
And also for Terrie,
Who makes dreams
come true*

Winnie's Wonderful Wheelchair

Winnie is a special girl with a wonderful wheelchair. She and her dog Waffles are perky - nothing ever gets them down.

Her wonderful wheelchair is magical to her, taking Winnie anywhere, and all her great adventures make her the talk of the town!

Yes! Winnie's wheelchair wonderfully wheels her everywhere.

And because those wheels of hers spin so very fast, Winnie's friends just stand and stare.

They call her wonder-
winnie@speedy.gogo
as she whizzes past!

But the thing that is
so much fun on
this very special day,
Is how Winnie's
wonderful wheelchair
races faster than a car!

And other times
Winnie's wonderful
wheelchair
wheels her from her
cozy home away....

To all her many
adventures
that are near or
very, very far.

On any spellbinding
occasion, Winnie's
wonderful wheelchair,
can take her speeding
faster than a jet plane.

Where she can
see weird and
wacky animals with
her in the air,
like dancing
armadillos, a
singing rainbow
bear, and a lovely
laughing crane.

Sometimes Winnie's
wonderful wheelchair
Is a spaceship sending
her through space.

To a mysterious
planet with funny
aliens there.

That join in
all her games.
"Catch Winnie!"
they all say.
It's such a
merry place.

On another day of
adventure, the
wheelchair
takes Winnie
sailing through the
swift and swirling
winds of a
blustery cyclone.

And there she passes
wild and stormy and
very exciting seas,
with Pirates who call,
"Ahoy there!" because
Winnie's never alone.

Her wonderful
wheelchair can
become a submarine,
bounding about
with brilliant sea
critters at play.

She ventures into deep watery realms where no one else has been.

Exploring dreamy life beneath the waves where only they can stay.

And Winnie and her
wonderful wheelchair,
can go down
deeper and deeper
to the deepest
ocean bay.

Exploring sunken
shipwrecks with
their treasures there.

As Winnie plays with
merry mermaids.
"Welcome, Winnie,"
they all say.

It is so amazing how
Winnie's wonderful
wheelchair can even
be a time machine,

Whirling back to the
dear old dinosaur
days with such
sensational sights.
Her favorite is to find
the place where the
stegosaurus has been.

Whoops! While
dodging those
flaming, flying
meteorites!

Winnie can even
fast forward to
glimpse how the
future will be,
where everyone
enjoys themselves
in the place where
no one walks.

A time where
wheels rule
and everyone
has fun, you see.
A time that's filled
with harmony when
everybody talks!

And, when Winnie's
delightful friends
begin to feel,
lonely and bored
and wonder what
to do today....

Wonderful Winnie
is always happy
to reveal,
an adventure that
lets her wheels
show the way!

Because when
Winnie is not
racing cars or
cruising in her
submarine
in the sea,

Winnie and her
friends get together
for a day of
fun and play,
and everyone can
see how she is as
happy as can be!

Winnie always shares
how she has a
two-wheeled pal
forever and a day.

Yes! All of Winnie's
friends do know,
and with big smiles
they get to say,
"Here's Winnie and
her wonderful
wheelchair.
Let's go! Hip hip…
Hip hip..
Hooooooray!!!!"

And Winnie and Waffles wheeled happily every after.

Winnie And Her Wonderful Wheelchair's Winning Week

It's a great start to a
normal week and it's
Monday,
Winnie, Waffles, and
her wonderful
wheelchair are
on their way!
Winnie is always bright
and full of hope,
always wanting to
help others cope.

Her wheelchair is
magic and Winnie
is so kind,
for each and every
problem, a solution
the dynamic trio are
sure to find.

When Winnie sees
someone like Billy
being pushed over by a
big bad bully,
it is something that
Winnie just doesn't
want to see.

So over to the pair
she speedily goes,
and Waffles
deliberately steps on
the big bad bully's toes!

And suddenly, the
bully seems to
understand.
"I'm sorry," he says
and shakes
Billy's hand.

On Tuesday, while
wheeling along with
her wonderful
wheelchair,
Winnie hears a sad and
hidden voice: "I have
no friends anywhere."

Wheeling rapidly
round the bend,
Winnie shouts: "I'll
be your friend!"

"Get on my
wheelchair, there's
no need to hide,
let's go for a merry
and magical ride."

Winnie and Florence
whizz around
all this day,
as crowds of children
come out to play.

There is lots of
laughter and
happiness as they go,
with loads of games
and frolicking - it is
a joyful show.

With all her new
friends this terrific
Tuesday,
Florence will no
longer be lonely
or hiding away.

Then, wheeling
along the windy
Wednesday,
Rosie cries: "Winnie,
please keep the
monster away!"

Rosie's eyes are
wide with fright:
"This monster is under
my bed every night!"

Winnie calmly comes
over: "I'm here to
help. Let me see."
"OK," says Rosie.
"Come and have a
sleep over with me."

That night, with
Winnie and Waffles,
it was exactly as
Rosie said.
There certainly is
something under
her bed!

Winnie wheels closer
and says: "Please come
out from there."
And a fluffy purple
creature rolls out
with big yellow
eyes that stare.

"I'm Lila. I'm here
at night, but not
in the day."
There is no fear now,
all are filled with fun
as they happily play.

But coming to a
halt on this
Thursday, early,
Winnie sees a
child who is all
hurley burley.

Freddie's frustration
fills him up and
makes him yell,
"He needs me,"
says Winnie.
"I can tell."

He is so frustrated
he's throwing things
in his garden
everywhere.
His family is so sad
as they simply
stand and stare.

Freddie jumps about
wearing a very
dark frown.
So Winnie wheels
closer: "Freddie,"
she says, "Let's
calm down."

Freddie can see his
frustration falling
away, but he's still
filled with agitation,
Then Winnie softly
soothes him until
she sees his
agitation shrinking
swiftly without
hesitation.

Then, it all vanishes.
"You won't see my
frustration
again this or any
other day,"
Freddie shouts as he
and his family smile
and they all exclaim,
"HOORAY!"

Friday is the day before
the weekend,
Winnie finds another
help-needing friend.

Sitting on his swing
with such a sorrowful
expression,
"I can't sing properly
and it causes me
depression."

"Well!" exclaims
Winnie, "I think
that's very wrong.
Let's sing together.
Come and pick
a song."

Bruce chooses
'Twinkle, twinkle
little star.'
Winnie joins in and
children come from
near and far.

Winnie and Bruce
sing many
lovely songs,
and all the other
children happily
sing along!

"Sing sure, sing strong,
for this is so right,
to make lives joyful, to
make lives bright!"

This week, Winnie
has helped her
five new friends,
there's a weekend
party at Winnie's and
the fun never ends!

They're all having
fun and capers and
happiness now,
and Waffles whirls as
the wheelchair
works wonders,
'WOW!'

The five new friends
have new friends
with them as well.
And everyone dances
about like in a
magic spell.

Could there be any better way
to celebrate this perfect week?
Than to remember Winnie
and her wonderful mystique?

Winnie and Her Wonderful Wheelchair's Fantastical Flower Show

Winnie waves to all the children gathering in her garden today, children are coming far and wide to see her flowers on display. The children gather round her, they are talking joyfully, Winnie's flowery surprise is a sight that only young eyes can see.

The stage is a flower bed and the floral blooms are the stars of the show.

Wearing petals of
colours borrowed
from sunset skies and
a bright rainbow.

As parents talk,
they're not aware of
this magical place
their children see,

Well now, the waiting's finally over, it's time to reveal the mystery.

"Welcome, my friends, Waffles and I give you a most magical floral treat...."

....let's all put our
hands together and
clap really loudly for
the Fantastical
Lavender Suite."

They hear tapping of a
tambourine and the
cymbal's chiming
sound, the
Wisteria sways in
a cloud of purple
blooms hanging
on the ground.

A pretty ping
Peony smiles shyly
as her leaves tap on
piano keys,
her sweet scent
drifts off into the
crowd as she plays
her melodies.

A blue face Iris with
fluffy yellow pollen
spheres strums the
strings of her ukulele,

"What delightful
music," the
children do agree,
"We'd love to hear
this daily!"

Next up, a group of
jazzy Hydrangea
blow tunes on their
saxophones today,
and with their
riveting refrain, they
swiftly blow all sorrows
very far, far away.

Foxglove are such happy souls on the heavenly harpsichord, they are harmonious and attractive, no one shan't ever be bored.

Mr. Delphinium proudly takes centre stage, he's really a budding rock star. The children all dance as he plays 'Monet Blue' on his fancy electric guitar,

While Waffles barks
as if to join in with
a 'Ha ha ha,' as he
watches the joyous
sight of the children
singing "Tra la la!"

The stunning pink
Roses prefer a more
classical tun as they
play on their violins,

And Waffles howls
along with their song,
he can't help the great
mood he is in.

Oh, wonderful
Wallflowers of tangerine,
playing gentle lullabies
on the harp,
each note we
hear is so soft on the
ear, yet the rhythm
is steady and sharp.

Snapdragons are
lively and snappy as
they tap out bold beats
on their drums,
the children can't
help but jump to their
feet as Winnie spins
to echoes that hum.

The Hollyhocks are
rather old-fashioned,
blooms, they wear large
petal hats on the go.

They love a bit of
history as they play
double bass on cellos
so nice and slow.

The flowers and their
instruments are all
playing merrily together
as the music flows.

And Winnie waves
her hands as the music
maestro who conducts
this beautiful show.

The lovely Lavender
blooms as all sing in
harmony, a choir of
purple petals in song.
Winnie's magical garden
is a talented orchestra,
which plays sweetly along.

Winnie beams as
Waffles and the
children jamboree with
flowers bopping too,
Oh! What a
blooming, musical,
fantastical,
harmonious hullabaloo!

Rainbows of magic
fill the air as children
and flowers sway
to and fro,

Winnie wheels
around to the musical
sounds as the laughing
children musically
go with the flow!

Moms and dads
smile at their happy
children as each
homeward bound
heads.

For it's time for
the musical flowers
to rest in their cosy
flower beds.

But for Winnie
and Waffles and
her Wonderful
Wheelchair, the
concert never ends,

For fabulous will forever be our magical, musical friends.

"Yes," Winnie says, "come what may, flowers will always brighten your day."

The End

Winnie and Her Wonderful Wheelchair's Terrific Time Trip

It's Winnie's birthday and she's in her wonderful wheelchair, bouncing around with her dog, Waffles, who's always there.
"Come on wonderful wheelchair, we're in for a special treat.
There are some amazing people we're about to meet."

Like Cleopatra, a noble and proud Egyptian queen, in the year 40 BC.
She is who Winnie and Waffles first amazingly see...

....along with the pyramids, the Sphinx, and the deep clear, almost endless Nile, "Have you seen my Mummy?" Cleo asks with a smile.

Then, dashing through time to 50 AD, the wheelchair, Winnie, and Waffles quickly fly, to see Boudicca in Britain as she chases the Romans rushing by.

"Hello, Winnie,"
Winnie hears
Boudicca happily say,
whilst the
Romans are rapidly
racing away!

The three have now
come to a coastal cliff
in the year 1588,
where Queen
Elizabeth
1st encounters the
Spanish Armada - Oh!
what a terrible fate.

"Welcome. Listen,
I am going to
make my brave
soldiers victoriously
sing. For I may be a
woman, but I have the
heart of a king."

Next, they meet
Jane Austin in
1843, as a girl
twelve-years-old,
she is already writing
tales that are still
terrifically told.

It turns out to be a
lovely sun-filled day,
As Jane, Winnie in
her wheelchair,
and Waffles
happily play.

They can't wait to meet
Florence Nightingale,
who cared for wounded
soldiers in the
Crimean war.
She is the next lady that
Winnie and Waffles
greet, walking with
her lamp in 1854.

"Look Waffles,"
says Winnie,
"She is so busy
that she hardly
sleeps, as she looks
after the needs of
all she so
carefully keeps."

Then, it's off to
1870, when Harriet
Tubman had her
underground railway -
Winnie, Waffles, and
the wonderful
wheelchair join them
as they all make
their way.

It is all so, so very happy to see, Harriet helping many, many people become free.

Votes for women! As Mary Poppins would agree, is what Emmaline Pankhurst, who livcd in 1913, wants to see.

"Hello Winnie.
Now, young lady,
I just have to say,
that I think that *you*
could be President
one day!"

"Now Waffles,
it's 1920, and
there's an
adventurous
journalist
named Nellie Bly,
who proved that
around the world
in 72 days she could
cross land and
sea and sky."

"Did you know Winnie," exclaims Nellie, "that my favourite colour is pink?!"
"Yes," replies Winnie. "And what you wrote about World War 1 made people really think."

"That x-ray looks like you Waffles," Winnie is amazed to find, how so many incredible things came from Marie Curie's mind.

"Ah, Winnie and Waffles, it's now 1928, so can you give me a hand, with my element Polonium, I've named it after my homeland - that is called Poland."

"Wow Waffles! It's 1934 and we're in a plane next to Amelia Earhart." This exciting trip gets Winnie and Waffles off to a thrilling start.

Amelia Earhart and her friends are flying so far and so very high - Amelia is known as an amazing explorer of the endless sky.

Frida Kahlo lived in 1935. She was a marvellous artist from Mexico. This is where Waffles and Winnie, in her wheelchair, now go.

"These paintings are incredible, such colour and such grace." "Gracias, Winnie," greets Frida, with a red-lipped smile spreading across her face.

Then, Winnie and Waffles find themselves sitting on a bus, where many, many people are making such a silly fuss.

The year is 1955
and Rosa Parks
won't move.
"I'll sit where
I belong!"
Winnie and Waffles
and more cheer
her right along!

Helen Keller was
taught by a miracle
worker, she was both
deaf and blind,
and is one of the most
incredible people one
could ever find.

Helen lived in
1960 and she said,
"Winnie, you don't
have to hear of see,
To be the best
that you can be."
And they all agree.

Now Winnie and
Waffles are on the
International Space
Station, "Wow!"
With Peggy Whitson,
the oldest lady
known in space,
then and also now.

Winnie, in her
wheelchair, and
Waffles witness Peggy
finishing her
record-breaking
walk in space -
In the year 2016,
Peggy Whitson - a
biochemist and master
chef, is so versatile, but
tells how space if her
very favourite place.

So, it's back home
again, and just
in time for tea,
Winnie has learnt
from everyone
that you.......

Don't need magic
or a wonderful
wheelchair to
make your dreams
come true -

Just stick to your
beliefs and you will
certainly see,

That you can be the very best 'you' that you can truly be!

Winnie and
Her Wonderful
Wheelchair's
Axolotl and Aardvark
Adventure

Winnie and Waffles
happily wake
this April morning,
always with so many
positive daily
prospects dawning,
because every seasonal
sunrise brings new
opportunity
for Winnie to visit
the folks in
her community.

Today, Winnie has
been invited to
Scientist Gwyneth
Green's - for she has
invented something
that must be seen!

Gwyneth shows her
five axolotls' new
'wet' suits with pride.
These allow them
to be out of
water and take her
aardvarks for a ride.

"You see Winnie,
each axolotl is
worth such a 'lotl!'

Not a fish, not a
mammal, not a
salamander,
they're rarer than a
perfectly huggable
Panda."

Winnie and Waffles
watch them ride
all around.
Aardvarks and axolotls
are such peculiar
pairs to be found.

"I'll have another
invention to
show you soon.
If it works, I'll be
over the moon."

A week later
Winnie and Waffles
hear a loud knocking
on the door.
"Come quickly,"
Gwyneth Green
says, "and I'll
tell you more."

Once at her house
she exclaimed, "It's a
terrible, terrible
day! My axolotls
and aardvarks have
vanished away!"

"I invented my
Mystical Travel Torch
with a 'portal' light.
But the cheeky
axolotls played
with it last night!"

"They, broke it and I
cannot mend it this
day or any other days.
It has sent my axolotl
and aardvark pairs in
weirdly separate ways!"

So, Winnie, Waffles,
and the wonderful
wheelchair,
fix it and set off
straight away
from there.

Following each
trace of travel light.
Knowing only they
can get it right.

Light leads them
through tall trees and
across a massive park.
There they spot the
first axolotl sitting
with its aardvark.

There, flowers dance
with big top-hatted
butterflies,
beneath beautiful
blush pink and
purple streaked skies.

Winnie sees them and
says, "Ok, let's go."
As a bright blue sun
starts to boldly glow.

Then on to number
two aboard a
talking boat.
In a world of water
he said, "I'm
Boaty - I'll keep
you afloat."

Here, crabs and
lobsters ride flashy
fish that can sing.
As they rescue pair two
amid the fishy din.

"Why 'hallo'
and 'goodbye,'"
says Boaty.
"And how well
you did do!"
As they head off
with that axolotl
and aardvark pair
number two.

Then on to find
the trickiest pair
number three.
Right in the middle
of many mythical
creatures we see.

Amid dragons, fairies, elves, and a very, very happy minotaur, as Winnie grabs pair number three and away they all soar.

The axolotls and aardvarks help find their fourth friends. In an amazing maze going round baffling bends.

Where the paths in
this maze keep
changing shape
and colour.
As away they all
speed, riding with
each other.

Whooshing through
flashing rainbows
they all go,
landing on white
clouds that
softly flow.

Where bird-people
swoop and dive.
From here Winnie and
the team bring back
pair number five!

All the axolotls
and aardvarks
are now
happily home.

Gwyneth Green
smiles: "Now no
need to roam.

For tomorrow is
Easter Sunday
Winnie and
Waffles. There will
be lots to do.

We'll all be busy
Easter egg
hunting the whole
day through!"

Winnie and Waffles
celebrate
Easter Sunday,

It is a joyous time
to show love in each
and every way!

After finding the
eggs, the aardvarks
and axolotls have
a ball,
while Winnie and
all her friends wish:
"A very happy
Easter to all."

The End

Winnie and Her Wonderful Wheelchair's Four Seasons Forever

The four seasons
remind me of
Nature's power.
Each season brings
fabulous beauty
to every hour.

Winnie thrives in
the four seasons'
enchanting variety,

Nature creates
changes and makes
everyone happy.

Winter swirls in
with snow elves
when winds are
icy chill.
Winnie and her
wheelchair
roll snowballs
down the hill.

Waffles and woolly
sheep bounce in
the snowy air,
like fluffy
clouds bleating with
fuzzy, windblown hair.

Snowflakes settle
on dark trees as
fragments of light.
Their branches
twinkle like stars
in the night.

"Come see, Waffles"
Winnie says.
"Look what
we've found!
You know, it takes a
snowflake two hours
to fall from a cloud to
the ground."

December 21st is
the shortest day
of the year.
It is the Winter
Solstice in
the Northern
Hemisphere.

Winnie watches as snowmen cycle to work on their 'icicles,' "Yes Waffles, Christmas frosty fun is very nice-icicles."

Lighting candles, we celebrate as the sun's warmth melts the snow. But for now it's raining and Teddy's staring through the window.

Against the glass
he's got his
furry chinny
chin chin.
"If it rains any harder,
Waffles, we'll have
to let him in!"

Then, Spring bursts
in, dancing
enthusiastically
as Winter goes,
and everything she
touches, turns to
fairy wings where
wonders glow!

Winnie watches gentle,
mild showers water
smiling flowers
each day,
past the months
of February and
March, to wetter
April and May.

Rain showers in the
sun, nicely wash both
houses and trees,
and, under umbrellas,
Winnie and Waffles
bob like ships at sea.

Floral fantasies come
to life as everything is
blossoming,
and they hum along
to children's choirs
sweetly singing.

The Native
Americans still so
clearly see:
*'In Spring Mother
Earth is pregnant -
tread lightly.'*

See how with new
life the empty
valleys flood,
as friendships
grow with each
opening bud.

And, in Spring,
Winnie's mum can't
let one day pass
without going out
and cutting the
green grass!

In Spring, we see
the growing
tree branches
start to sway,
Sway - swing,
swing - sway
throughout each
live-long day.

Summer sparkles,
as sunshine glistens
on streams.
Merry children laugh,
as laughing
flowers gleam.

As they play, Waffles and Winnie stay cool by ice cream eating, while Teddy's bear-conditioning keeps him from overheating!

Great bursts of birds, baby dragons, and flumes of butterflies, form golden swirls around Winnie under bright blue skies.

Summer Solstice is the
longest day, on June
twenty and one.
Come on everyone,
let's go out and have
some evening fun.

Summer is brilliant
for the beach
and the sea.
Winnie and Waffles
discover curious
crabs and starfish
and throw a frisbee.

Winnie and Waffles
and their friends
make a great
sandcastle
building team.
Yes, summer days
shimmer away like
a fairytale dream.

Everyone's having
great fun in
bright flip flops
As the sun shines
high and never
really drops!

It's Summer's warmth
that wraps around
like a mother's arms,
so it seems.
Slumber, Oh Summer,
like Shakespeare's
'Midsummers Night's
Dreams.'

And then, in comes
Autumn, that
some call Fall.
Still, it's Harvest time,
with rainbow
colours overall,
Winnie, Waffles, and
Forest Sprites stare up
at deciduous trees
who are weeping red
and gold tear-leaves in
the gentle breeze.

Like a magician,
Autumn-Fall
waves its wand
and all fruits
flourish – of
which we're
especially fond!

Cherry pie and juicy
blackberries, "Yum!"
Winnie and Waffles say.
And always remember,
without a November you
can't have a May.

Fall equinox –
September 23rd,
when day and night
are the same.
"I wonder," Winnie
says, "if this is
all part of Autumn's
playful game."

The wind blows,
dragons glide, and
the skies are
darkly bright,
"Come on Waffles,
grab the tail and let's
all go fly a kite."

Is this the last page? Oh no! How did this book go so fast?
Winnie and Waffles say, "Four seasons will forever last."
So, let's all enjoy Autumn/Fall, Winter, Summer and Spring!
And the magical memories that each season may bring.

Winnie and Her Wonderful Wheelchair's Winter Wonderland Adventure

We know Christmas
comes but once
a year,
yet all year-round
Winnie brings
good cheer.
With her wonderful
wheelchair
and Waffles she goes,
spreading joy - like
sunshine on days of
wind-swirling snows.

Noel will soon be
knocking on this
season's door,
and, as Winnie is
busy decorating, a
tiny light reveals more.

"Winnie, we know
that helping is
your goal.
Please come to
our rescue at the
North Pole!"

As they arrive, an
Ice Fairy flutters
into view and says,
"Winnie, do
come along.
The silly Hurrooo
has released all the
spells that have
all gone wrong!"

"Christmas
is coming and
the turkeys are
getting fat,
but now we're in
more of a flap than
the flappiest bat!"

So, zooming over
ice and sea, Winnie's
wheelchair flies,
to help who they
can under the
North Pole skies.

Waffles is excited as they travel to this winter wonderland - and, like Winnie, he's always there to lend a helping hand.

In this mythical Arctic, the horizon is an array of dazzling fireworks, where around every ice mound magical mystery lurks.

And, a polar bear,
raising his top hat says,
"How do you do?
We are all very
pleased to
welcome you."

"Here, magic that
has 'gone off' was
put in barrels and
sealed away.
But the
nosey Hurrooo has
found and opened
them today!"

Winnie sees the
absent-minded
Hurrooo wandering
around.
He looks rather
puzzled by
all the chaos
he's found.

The naughty magic
is causing everyone
such worry.
For the elves are
daydreaming and are
not in any hurry.

'Oh, no!' The reindeer have all lost their ability to fly. 'Nothing is working properly!' the panicked penguins cry.

"It's such a kerfuffle!" the Ice Fairy says. "That foolish Hurrooo has left poor Santa clueless. He knows not what to do!"

Winnie and Waffles watch Santa dodging and dashing about, trying frantically to put back all the spells that have gotten out.

"Don't worry, let's be positive," Winnie says, "just BELIEVE. Me and Waffles will help sort all these things out before Christmas Eve."

They grab the stray magic and seal it in the barrels nice and firm - no matter how those wayward spells might sparkle, shimmer, and squirm.

"Wait!" exclaims Santa, "Things won't be normal for a day or two. It's Christmas tomorrow. What *am* I going to do?"

Winnie puts the
polar bear to work
assisting the puffins
who pack.
They need to get
all the presents
ready, there's no
looking back.

All the while, the
silly Hurrooo stares
at the Ice Fairy's
wand a-tapping,

She's making sure all those presents have a magical wrapping!

Everyone watches snow butterflies that flutter with crystal wings,

Sprinkling sparkles
and shimmers
onto all of the things.

"The presents are
superb!" Santa shouts.
"But what now?
We have reindeer that
cannot fly, so please
do tell me how?"

"Don't worry, Santa,"
Winnie says,
"Just be a merry man!
For Waffles and
I have a most
Christmassy plan!"

Then, Winnie and
her wonderful
wheelchair save
the day,
as she pulls Santa
and all in his
ho, ho, ho, so
special sleigh.

Waffles sits beside
the jolly man and
wags his tail in
the air,
as they magically
deliver presents to
children everywhere.

Yes, in the North Pole
they say the sky is filled
with fireworks,

And you can bet
around every
corner magical
mystery lurks.

And so, as the
Ice fairy brings
glittering silver to
snowflakes that fall,

We wish a very
'Merry Winnie Noel'
to you all ...

For the Christmas
spirit is a special gift
we each can give,
to fill our lives with
wonder every day that
we all shall live.

The End

David R Morgan lives in England. He is a talented full-time teacher and writer.

He has written music journalism, poetry and children's books. His books for children include : 'The Strange Case of William Whipper-Snapper', three 'Info Rider' books for Collins and 'Blooming Cats' which won the Acorn Award and was animated for television. He has also written a Horrible Histories biography : 'Spilling The Beans On Boudicca' and stories for Children's anthologies.

For the last 5 years he has been working on his Soundings Project with his son Toby, performing his own poetry/writing to Toby's original music. This work is on YouTube, Spotify and Soundcloud.